may my heart always be open to little
birds who are the secrets of living
— From E.E. Cummings, poem 53

Design & layout: Pascale Rosier

First American edition published in 2012 by Enchanted Lion Books, 20 Jay Street, M-18, Brooklyn, NY 11201. Translation © 2012 by Enchanted Lion Books, LLC. Translated by Claudia Zoe Bedrick. First published in Switzerland © 2010 by Editions La Joie de lire S.A. as *Les Oiseaux*. All rights reserved in accordance with the Copyright Act of 1956 as emended. A CIP record is on file with the Library of Congress. ISBN 978-1-59270-118-6. Printed in China in December 2011 by Toppan Leefung.

LITTLE BIRD

Germano Zullo
Albertine

ENCHANTED LION BOOKS
New York

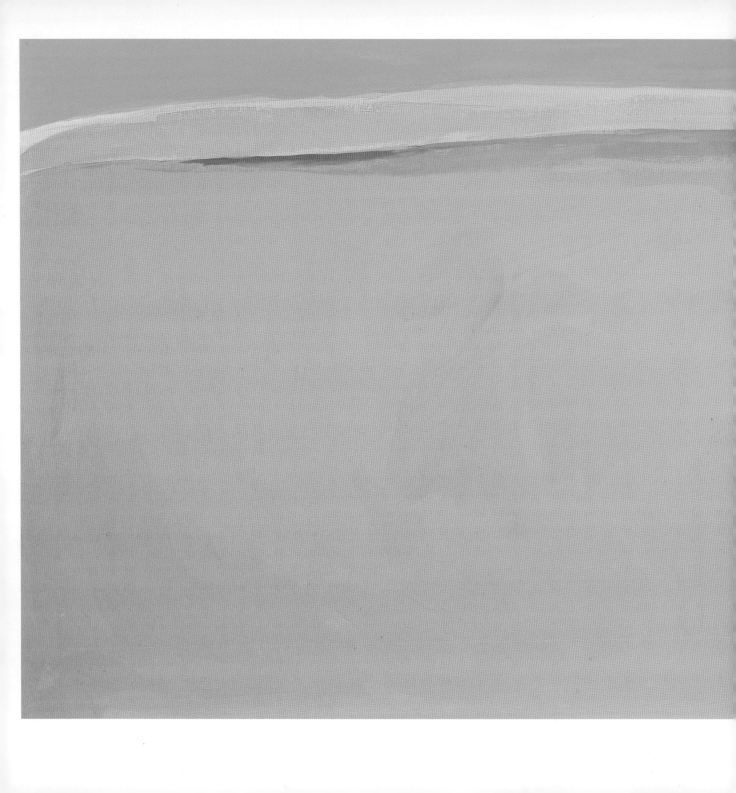

Some days are different.

One could **alm**ost believe that one day is just like another.

But some have something a little more.

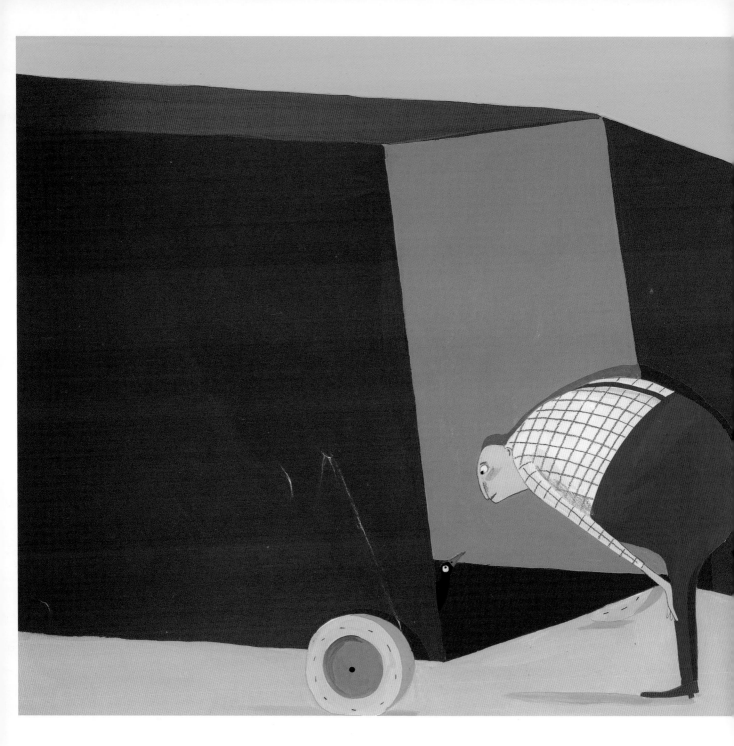

Nothing much.

Just a small thing.

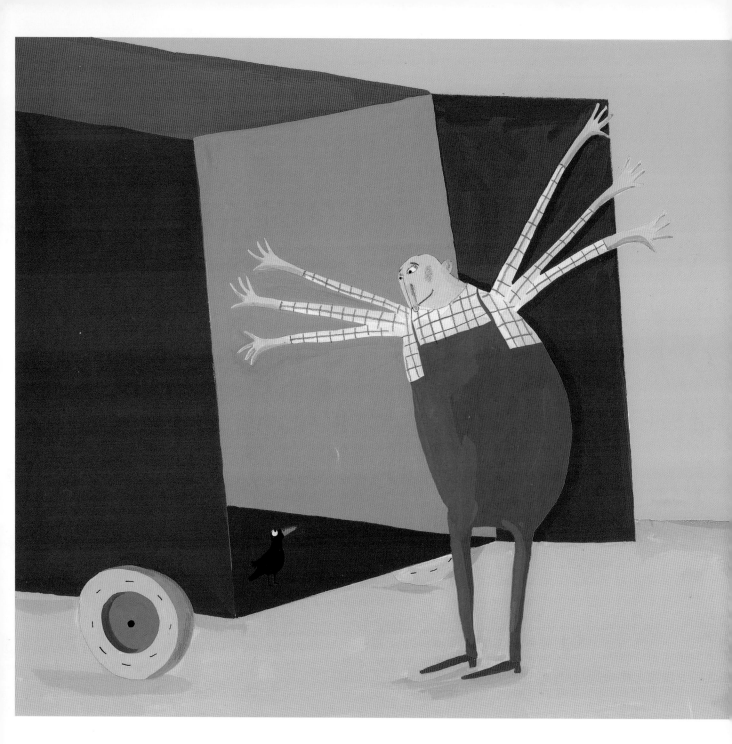

Tiny.

Most of the time we don't notice these things.

Because little things are not made to be noticed.

They are there to be discovered.

When we take the time to look for them...

the small things appear.

Here or there.

Tiny.

But suddenly so present...

they seem enormous.

The small things are treasures.

True treasures.

There are no greater treasures than the little things.

One is enough to enrich the moment.

Just one is enough to change the world.